The Happy Egg

Story by RUTH KRAUSS

Pictures by CROCKETT JOHNSON

SCHOLASTIC BOOK SERVICES
NEW YORK • TORONTO • LONDON • AUCKLAND • SYDNEY • TOKYO

More books by RUTH KRAUSS and CROCKETT JOHNSON

Is This You?*
The Carrot Seed*
How to Make an Earthquake

*Available through Scholastic Book Services.

 This edition is published by Scholastic Book Services, a division of Scholastic Magazines, Inc.

23 22 21 20 19 18 17 16 15 14 13 12 6 7 8 9/7 01/8

07

SEE-SAW books

Printed in the U.S.A.

The Happy Egg

There was a little little bird.

It was just born.
It still was an egg.

It couldn't walk.
It couldn't sing.
It couldn't fly.

It could just get sat on.

So it got sat on
and sat on

and sat on
and sat on

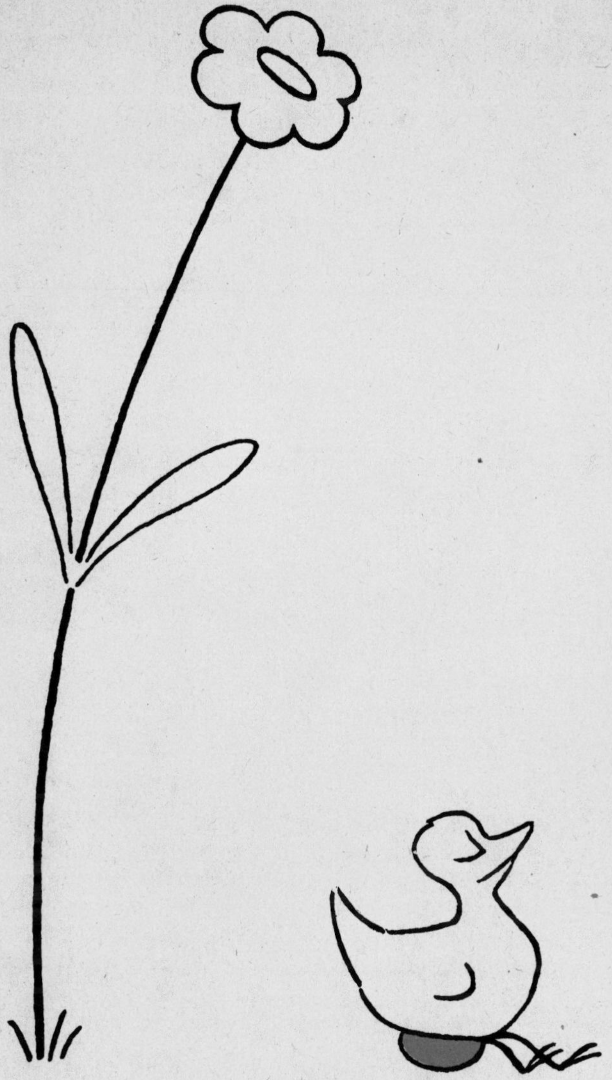

and sat on
and sat on
and sat on

and sat on.

And one day,

peep

POP! Out it came.

It could walk.

It could sing.

It could

fly.

It could someday sit on
other happy eggs.

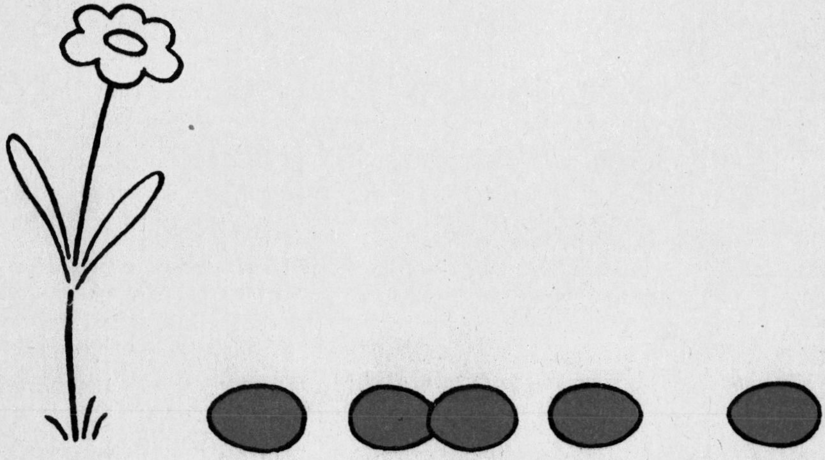